W9-DCG-172

WELCOME TO THE WORLD
OF
Geronimo Stilton

Published by Sweet Cherry Publishing Limited
Unit 36, Vulcan House,
Vulcan Road,
Leicester, LE5 3EF
United Kingdom

First published in the UK in 2020

2 4 6 8 10 9 7 5 3 1

ISBN: 978-1-78226-534-4

Geronimo Stilton names, characters and related indicia are copyright, trademark
and exclusive license of Atlantyca S.p.A. All Rights Reserved.
The moral right of the author has been asserted.

Text by Geronimo Stilton
Art Director: Iacopo Bruno
Graphic Designer: Andrea Cavallini / theWorldofDOT
Original cover illustration by Roberto Ronchi (graphics) and Andrea Cavallini (colour)
Concept of illustration by Larry Keys, produced by Claudio Cernuschi and Maria De Filippo
Initial and final page illustrations by Roberto Ronchi and Ennio Bufi, MAD5 (design) and Studio
Parlapà and Andrea Cavallini (colour). Map illustrations by Andrea Da Rold and Andrea Cavallini
Graphics by Merenguita Gingermouse and Zeppola Zap
Cover layout and typography by Margot Reverdiau
Interior layout and typography by Rhiannon Izard
© 2003-2016 Edizioni Piemme S.p.A., Palazzo Mondadori – Via Mondadori, 1 – 20090 Segrate
© 2020 UK edition, Sweet Cherry Publishing
International Rights © Atlantyca S.p.A. – via Leopardi 8, 20123 Milano, Italy
Translation © 2005 by Atlantyca S.p.A.

Original title: *L'isola del tesoro fantasma*
Based on an original idea by Elisabetta Dami

www.geronimostilton.com/uk

*Stilton is the name of a famous English cheese. It is a registered trademark of the Stilton Cheese Makers'
Association. For more information go to www.stiltoncheese.com*

No part of this book may be stored, reproduced or transmitted in any form or by any means,
electronic or mechanical, including photocopying, recording, or by any information storage and
retrieval system, without written permission from the copyright holder. For information regarding
permissions, contact Atlantyca S.p.A. – foreignrights@atlantyca.it – www.atlantyca.com

Not to be sold outside the UK

www.sweetcherrypublishing.com

Printed and bound in Turkey
T.IO006

Geronimo Stilton

SHIPWRECK ON PIRATE ISLAND

Sweet Cherry

But Won't It Be ... Dangerous?

I was working peacefully in my office one morning when my sister burst through the door. Thea is the special correspondent at The Rodent's Gazette. What is the Gazette? Oops. Sorry, mouse fans. I forgot to introduce myself. My name is Stilton, **GERONIMO STILTON**.

I run a newspaper called The Rodent's Gazette. It is the most popular daily on Mouse Island.

"**Drop everything**, Geronimo!" Thea demanded. "We're going on a mini **holiday**!"

I shook my head. I was way too busy. I had to meet with the printer. I had to meet with the photographer. I had to meet with the cafeteria mouse. I had found a tuft of fur in my macaroni and cheese last week. **Yuck!**

Just then, my favourite nephew, Benjamin, appeared. "Uncle, have you heard the news?" he squeaked happily. "We're all going on holiday! I'm so **excited**!" This is going to be the best holiday of my whole life!"

How could I say no to my dear, sweet nephew? "Well, all right," I agreed. "Why don't we go to the Soft Squeak resort? It's on a **beautiful**, relaxing island …"

Before I could continue, my sister interrupted me. "Forget Soft Squeak, **Gerry Berry**. That place is for senior citizens," she scoffed. "We're going to the PIRATE ISLANDS. White beaches, crystal-clear water, and jungles filled with **WILD ANIMALS**! There are tigers, pythons, and even gigantic tarantulas!"

9

I shivered. "Umm, well the white beaches and crystal-clear water sounds great, but won't all those wild animals be **DANGEROUS**?"

Thea snickered. "Oh, **Geronimoid**, stop being such a scaredy-mouse!" she scolded. "Go pack your suitcase. We'll meet at the airport in twenty minutes!"

Twenty minutes? I barely had time to comb my fur!

10

THE PIRATE ISLANDS GUIDEBOOK

Luckily, I remembered to pack a guidebook on the **PIRATE ISLANDS**. I like to read about the places I visit.

I read about the pirates, too. This is what I learned:

The Pirate Code

Many believe that pirates broke every law known to mice. But that is not exactly true. Pirates did obey some laws, but only ones that were established aboard their own ship. For example:

The loot is to be divided equally among all pirates.

No pirate is allowed to gamble.

Every pirate must always be ready for battle.

No women or children are allowed on board.

Whoever steals or flees from combat will be punished by death.

Privateers, Buccaneers and Filibusters

After Christopher Columouse landed in America, there was an outbreak of piracy along the Caribbean coast and in the Antilles. There were several types of pirates.

Privateers were sailors who carried a letter, given by their king, authorising them to attack enemy ships. In exchange for this document, they gave half of their booty to their sovereign.

Buccaneers were European pirates who attacked Spanish ships and settlements in the West Indies.

Filibusters were pirates of English, French, and Dutch origin who operated in the Caribbean.

Help, Pirate Overboard !

It seems incredible, but often pirates did not know how to swim. They prided themselves on dominating the seas without ever taking a bath.

For example, the pirate Bartholomew Portugues did not know how to swim, so he fled from a prison ship by floating to shore on a raft made of kegs.

The Jolly Rodger

Whenever someone saw a pirate flag approaching, he would be so frightened that more often than not he would surrender without a fight.

Every commander had his own personal flag. These are the most famous:

John Rackham (died 1720)
"Calico Jack"

This English pirate liked to dress in calico. He would attack local merchants and fishing vessels in the Caribbean. Despite the pirate rule about no women on board, Calico Jack had not one but two women pirates disguised as men among his crew.

Bartholomew Roberts (1682-1722) "Black Bart"

This English pirate was probably the most successful pirate in history. He captured four hundred vessels and operated off the coast of South America and in the West indies. He never drank or gambled and always went to bed early.

Henry Avery (1665-1728) "Long Ben"

This Englishman was a pirate for only one year, but in that time he captured riches and booty from English, Indian, and Danish ships off the coasts of Africa and India. He is probably the only well-known pirate who was not killed in battle or ever caught for his crimes. But he died penniless after losing all his booty on land.

Edward Teach (died 1718) "Blackbeard"

This Englishman turned pirate in 1713 and preyed on ships off the coast of the Carolinas and Virginia. He captured a large French merchantman, equipped her with forty guns, and renamed her Queen Anne's Revenge.

PIRATE ABC'S

Aft: Towards the rear or stern of a boat.

Aweigh: The position of the anchor as it is raised clear of the bottom of the sea.

Batten down: Secure hatches and loose objects both within the hull and on deck.

Below: Beneath the deck.

Booty: Riches or valuables taken by force.

Bow: The forward part of a boat.

Bridge: The part of the ship from which the vessel is steered and its speed controlled.

Chart: A map used by navigators.

Course: The direction in which a boat is steered.

Deck: The permanent covering over a compartment, hull, or any part of the ship.

Doubloon: A gold coin once used in Spain and Spanish America.

Forward: Toward the bow of a boat.

Galley: The kitchen area of a boat.

Halyards: Lines used to hoist or lower sails or flags.

Jolly Rodger: A pirate flag, usually with a skull-and-crossbones design.

Knot: A measure of speed equal to one nautical mile (6,076 feet) per hour.

Logbook: The ship's diary, used to record weather conditions, speed, and any relevant information about navigation and crew.

Mast: A vertical pole used to support sails and their rigging.

Port: The left side of a boat when one is looking forward.

Rudder: A vertically hinged plate of metal or wood mounted at the stern of a vessel, which is used to steer its course.

Sail: A piece of cloth that catches or directs the wind and powers a vessel.

Sea Dog: An experienced sailor.

Stern

Shiver me timbers: An expression of surprise of disbelief. When a ship strikes a rock hard, her timbers shiver.

Shrouds: Ropes used to support the masts.

Starboard: The right side of a boat when one is facing forward.

Stern: The rear end of a boat.

Walk the plank: To be forced to walk over the side of a ship into the sea.

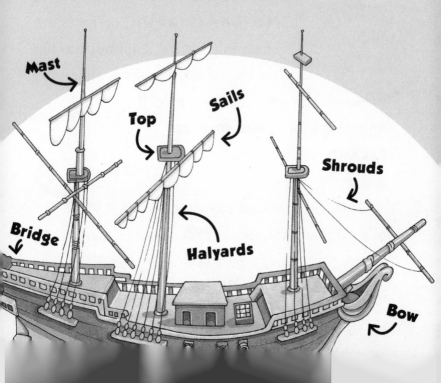

LITTLECOCOA

I continued to read the guidebook: "Some islands are no longer inhabited. One such is **LITTLECOCOA**, on which only one coconut tree grows. On the island of **FIN'S REVENGE**, the waters near the beaches are infested with

FIN'S REVENGE

FEROCIOUS SHARKS. Around the isle of **MOTORMELTDOWN**, currents are so strong that the ships need to run the engine at full power so they don't crash against the cliff.

MOTORMELTDOWN

And then there's **NO MOUSE'S ISLAND**, an extremely small and uncharted island.

NO MOUSE'S ISLAND

"Finally, the farthest and wildest of all of them is the island **NO** aeroplane dares to fly to and where **NO** ship ever docks, and where **NO** on would dream of going ... the island of **THUMP FLOP**, where

18

THUMP FLOP

numerous plop birds live. Here, according to legend, a pirate hid a treasure right on the –"

My reading was interrupted by someone squeaking my name. It was my cousin Trap. "Shake a paw, **Germeister**!" he shrieked. Everyone in the airport turned and stared.

One thing you should know about Trap. He is the **loudest**, most **obnoxious** mouse in the world! Even worse, he loves to pick on me. I cringed. So much for a relaxing holiday. **I would be lucky if I made it home with all of my whiskers!**

A Most Bizarre Mouse

The plane landed thirteen hours later. My stomach was in knots, and not nautical knots, if you know what I mean! Did I mention I'm **AFRAID** of flying?

A small hydroplane was waiting to take us to a place called **LOOT ISLAND**. According to my guidebook, the island was small and totally uncivilised. That mean no lights. No running water. No cheese logs by the pool. I sighed. Oh how I *love* a **CHEDDAR CHEESE LOG**.

My thoughts were interrupted by a most bizarre-looking rodent. He had lots of **CURLY** black hair and was dressed in purple shorts and a neon yellow shirt with red **hearts**. Around

his neck hung a huge gold medal with the word **SCRAM!** printed on it.

PIRATE ISLANDS

A = PAWSOFFTHEGOLD
B = FIN'S REVENGE
C = ANCHOR ARCH
D = MOTORMELTDOWN
E = BUCCANEER'S COVER
F = NO MOUSE LAND
G = LITTLECOCOA
H = TREASURE TRAP
I = WINDY POINT
J = SAILOR'S DELIGHT
K = ANCHORS AWEIGH ISLE
L = LOOT ISLAND
M = CAPTAIN'S CURSE
N = PARROT ISLE
O = THUMP FLOP
X = BURIED TREASURE

"Yo, **Mousey Mouse**!" he greeted me and stuck out one chubby paw. I noticed a shark-toothed bracelet dangling from his wrist. "The name's **ROUGH RAT RICKY**, but everyone calls me **BOUNCER**," he announced.

He squeezed my paw so hard, my eyes nearly popped out of my **fur**. **RANCID RAT HAIRS!** That mouse had some shake. He was crushing every bone in my paw! I wouldn't be able to write for weeks!

I was about to complain when I noticed his tattoos. One his left arm, there was a picture of a hideous dragon. On his right arm, there was a **FEROCIOUS CAT** with blood dripping from its jaws.

I gulped. Yes, they were only tattoos – but they looked so real! What kind of mouse liked such **TERRIFYING** tattoos? I stared up at Bouncer. That's when I saw his ear. It looked like it had been chewed by a **CAT**! No, I wasn't going to mess with this rodent.

Just then, Bouncer smacked me hard on the back. My whiskers nearly flew off my snout. "Ready to leave, **Mousey Mouse**?" he chuckled.

I tried to squeak, but no sound came out. **Bouncer had knocked the wind out of me.**

Scram! Move It! Get Lost!

BOUNCER bounded onto the hydroplane. He patted a photo on the dashboard with his stubby paw. It was a picture of an older female mouse with hair just like Bouncer's. "Hi, Momsy Womsy!" he cooed. He blew the picture a kiss. Then he stared at the controls. **"Frozen cheddar cheese pop!"** he shrieked suddenly. "I've forgotten how to turn on the engine!"

My jaw hit the ground. "Wh-wh-what d-d-did you s-s-s-say?" I stammered.

Bouncer winked at me. "Just pulling your paw, **Mousey Mouse!**" he chuckled.

BOUNCER'S MUM

I grabbed my cousin's paw. "Couldn't you have found a normal pilot?" I asked softly. "This one is so **strange.** Won't it be dangerous flying with him?"

Trap just smirked. "All pilots are strange. Look at your sister," he remarked. "She's one of the **strangest** mice I know."

Thea **JUMPED** to her paws. My sister is a licensed pilot. She even has her own plane.

"How **DARE** you!" she squeaked at Trap. Before I knew it, the two of them were at each other's throats.

I signed. Meanwhile, Bouncer began preparing for take-off. First he checked the controls. Then he checked his hair with a pocket mirror. "Looking good!"

I stared anxiously out the window. The sky was growing cloudy. **VERY CLOUDY.**

"The weather doesn't look so great. Won't it be **DANGEROUS** flying in all of these clouds?" I asked Thea.

She just scoffed. "I'm sure Bouncer called the control tower. They check on the weather. If they say we can leave, then we leave. Don't be such a scaredy-mouse, **Germeister**."

I couldn't help it. The sky was getting **darker** and **darker**. It looked like we were about to fly into a big storm. Was it a thunderstorm? **I HATE THUNDERSTORMS**. At home, I hide under my bed when there is a thunderstorm.

Suddenly, Bouncer stuck his head out of the window. He waved a paw at everybody on the runway. "**SCRAM!** Move it! Get lost!" he shrieked. Then he turned on the plane, and we **shot off** into the sky.

As soon as we were airborne, he smacked his forehead with his paw. "**CHEESE NIBLETS!**" he squeaked. "I forgot to get fuel!"

My stomach dropped. "No f-f-fuel?" I stammered.

Bouncer roared with laughter. "Just pulling your paw, **Mousey Mouse**!"

I chewed my whiskers. Oh, why did I agree to come on this **AWFUL** holiday? I could have been relaxing at the Soft Squeak Resort. I could

have been playing shuffleboard. I could have been getting a **massage**. Instead I was listening to a crazy mouse telling warped jokes.

This wasn't a holiday. It was a NIGHTMARE!

I Told You So ...

After an hour, the sky turned completely **black**. The plane began to **SHAKE VIOLENTLY**. The wind **ROARED**. It **screamed**. It wound my tail up in knots. Oh, no, that wasn't the wind. That was me. I wind my tail when I'm nervous. I really should break the habit. Thea says it makes your fur fall out. I hope she's wrong. Have you ever seen a mouse with no fur? Let me tell you, it is not a pretty sight.

Bouncer's voice interrupted my thoughts. "Control tower, what's the deal with the weather?" he shouted.

The radio crackled. "Tornado ... headed ... right ... for ... you!!!" a voice screamed. **"EMERGENCY!"**

Everyone turned as pale as a ball of mozzarella. Well, everyone except me. That's because I was already pale. The blood had **frozen** under my fur the minute I'd stepped on board!

"A **TORNADO** is coming!" Bouncer announced. I felt faint. "I told you so!" I squeaked. **"I told you that it was dangerooooooooooous!"**

Nose Down Into the Deep Blue Waves

I helped Benjamin put on a life jacket.

No one was talking. How unusual. Normally, you can't get the Stilton family to stop squeaking. Everyone stared worriedly at the sky. It grew **DARKER** and **DARKER**.

The wind blew furiously. The plan lurched and swayed. **Swish ... swishh ... swishhh ...**

I held on to Benjamin's tiny paw for dear life.

"Don't worry little nephew," I whispered. "We'll be just fine." I hoped he couldn't hear my teeth chattering.

Or see my **fur** standing on end. Or feel my paw trembling. **RAT-MUNCHING RATTLESNAKES!** I was scared silly!

Suddenly, Bouncer pointed the plane's nose toward land.

"Hang on!" he screamed. "I'm going to try to make an emergency landing!"

The wind grew **STRONGER** and **STRONGER**. The waves grew closer and closer.

Seconds later, a gust of wind sent the plane **plunging into the deep blue waves.**

GLUB ... BLUB, BLUB, BLUB!

The plane crashed into the sea with a loud **SPLASH**. Instantly we began to sink. **GLUB ... BLUB, BLUB, BLUB!**

We tried to open the door. It wouldn't budge.

Then I remembered something I had read in one of my favourite books. In the book, the hero accidentally drives off a bridge. His car sinks **UNDERWATER**. The water pressure is too strong for him to escape. He has to wait until the car goes completely under.

Before long, the water had covered our plane. I pushed with all of my strength. **And the door opened!** Isn't reading amazing?

I took a deep breath. Then I grabbed Benjamin's paw and hurled myself out into the water. It was **freezing!**

I started swimming. The water was darker than my

**We tried to
open the door** ...

... **but only when
the plane was
filled with water** ...

... **then we were able to escape !**

mouse hole at **MIDNIGHT**. I couldn't see my own fur in front of my face. But I could see **bubbles**. They were coming from my mouth. I followed them up to the surface.

"WE MADE IT!" I spluttered, giving Benjamin a hug.

Thea and Trap popped up next to me. But there was no sign of Bouncer.

I looked around and spotted a small island not too far away. We swam to shore. Then we collapsed onto the sand.

WATER dripped down my whiskers. I was so tired, I couldn't move. That was a good thing, because **I wanted to strangle my sister for bringing me on this nightmare holiday!**

NOTHING CAN STOP THE STILTON FAMILY!

The **sun** was about to rise. I was feeling hopeful.

Then I heard someone sobbing. It was Trap. "What if we're trapped here forever?" he **moaned**. "I'll never go to another mouseball game again. I'll never see my friends. I'll never eat another cheddar melt at the **All U Can Eat Cheese Palace**."

Did I mention that my cousin loves to eat? And eat ... **and eat** ...

Thea rolled her eyes. "Get a grip, Trap," she squeaked. "We Stiltons never give up."

Benjamin smiled. "Aunt Thea's right, Cousin Trap," he nodded. "Nothing can stop the Stilton family!"

With a sigh, Trap got a grip on himself. Then we twisted our tails together and shouted, **"NOTHING CAN STOP THE STILTON FAMILY!"**

We came up with a list of chores. Trap was in charge of getting the food. Thea gathered wood to light the **FIRE**. Benjamin made little skirts out of palm leaves so we'd have something to wear (our clothes were **SOAKING WET**). And I built a shelter under a coconut tree.

It was a **HARD** day. The sun **roasted** my fur. The wind tangled my whiskers. My paws sprouted a thousand blisters. Well, OK, maybe not a thousand blisters. But you get the picture. It was hard work.

I stared at the ocean. It looked so cool and inviting. But I was **afraid**. What if a shark attacked me? What if a jellyfish stung me? What if my grass skirt floated away?

Just then, something plopped onto my head.

Seconds later, there were more plops.

PLOP! PLOP! PLOP!

The sky had filled with a swarm of birds. They looked just like seagulls. **"Squawk, squawk,**

37

squawk!" the birds called.

Benjamin quickly handed out little umbrellas made of leaves. He was getting pretty good with those leaves. First the skirts. Then the umbrellas. What next? Shirts? Ties? Maybe someday Benjamin would grow up to be a designer. "Never leaf home without your Benjamin Stilton." **Hmm ... maybe he was onto something.**

I Am Rodent,
Hear Me Squeak!

Just then, another **plop** hit my umbrella. It reminded me of the guidebook on the PIRATE ISLANDS. It talked about the plop birds on an island called **THUMP FLOP**.

"I know where we are!" I cried excitedly. "We're on Thump Flop Island. I read about it in the guidebook. It said the island had plants and edible fruits."

Thea grinned. "Good work, **Gerry Berry**," she squeaked. "I guess it pays to have a bookmouse for an older brother sometimes."

I was about to remind her that my name is not **Gerry Berry** when I remember something else. I had read a few more interesting things in that guidebook.

"In **ANCIENT** times, pirates brought their

GOLD and riches to the **PIRATE ISLANDS**. Many treasures are still buried there. There are also many *GHOSTS* on the islands. The ghost of the famous pirate Silverpaw wanders the beaches on the island of **THUMP FLOP**. His ship was said to have mysterious powers. It could appear and disappear in the blink of an eye."

That night, I curled up in a big palm leaf to sleep. It wasn't easy. I kept thinking about pirates and ghosts and disappearing ships. *Don't be such a scaredy-mouse,* I scolded myself. I sang a little song to give myself courage: "I am brave. I am strong. I am rodent, hear me **SQUEAK!**"

My cousin Trap mimicked me in a sing-song voice. **"I am brave. I am strong. I am rodent, hear me snore!"**

YOU HAVE A LEECH ON YOUR FACE!

The next day, we decided to **explore** the island. We headed down a long, sandy path. It led into a thick mangrove **FOREST**. My paws sank into the damp sand. It was hard to walk.

Suddenly, I noticed something odd. **HUGE HOLES** were opening up in the sand. The holes were filled with **gigantic crabs**. Their pincerlike claws swiped at us as we scampered by.

"HOLEY CHEESE!" I cried out. My heart began to race. Sweat rolled down my fur. Do you like crabs? I don't. They always look angry. I hate those razor-sharp claws. And their beady little eyes look so sinister.

No one else seemed to be bothered by the crabs. Trap was even humming a silly tune.

Just then, something slimy and wet hit me in the face.

"A **LEECH!** Geronimo, you have an **ENORMOUSE** leech on your face!" hollered trap.

I began to see stars. **"Heeeeeelp!"** I shrieked. I ripped the wet leech off my face. Then I stared at it in my paw.

"B-b-but this isn't a leech," I blabbered. "It's a wet handkerchief."

Trap was jumping up and down and all around me, **roaring with laughter**.

I should have known. Have I told you my cousin loves to play tricks on me?

"Ha-ha-ha! You fell for it, **Germeister**!" he spluttered. "You're so easy to fool. It's like taking **Cheesy Chews** from a mouseling!"

I ran after him. "If I catch you, you'll never eat another **Cheesy Chew** again!" I shouted.

44

BIGGER THAN FIFTY SUMO RAT WRESTLERS!

Trap was still **laughing** as he ran down the path. Then he turned to make a face at me. That's when his face went pale.

"Ge-Ge-Geronimo ... d-d-don't move ..." he stuttered. "There's a **GIGANTIC C-C-CRAB** behind you!"

I snorted. You can fool this mouse sometimes, but I'm no **CHEESEBRAIN.** I mean, I wasn't born yesterday. I know when someone is pulling my paw. "Enough kidding around, Trap," I said, **laughing**. "I known there's no giant crab."

My cousin's eyes were nearly popping out of their sockets. I had to give it to him. He really did look **scared**. I wondered if he had been taking acting lessons in his spare time.

"I am not kidding, Geronimo," he whispered. "Look behind you."

I rolled my eyes. I was getting tired of these silly tricks. Still, I turned around anyway. "See, I told you ..." I began.

But I didn't get any further. That's because for once, Trap wasn't joking. I was face-to-face with a gigantic, enormouse, **MEGA-HUGE CRAB!**

I had never seen anything like it. This crab was bigger than fifty sumo rat wrestlers!

Remain calm, I told myself.

I took a small step backward, then another. The crab kept its beady little eyes trained on me.

Only a few more pawsteps and I could dive into the **WATER**. I'd be safe there.

Suddenly, my cousin sneezed.

In a flash, the crab stretched out its claw and lifted me into the air.

"HeeeeeeeeeeLP!" I yelled. The blood rushed to my **FURRY** head.

Thea and Benjamin stuck their heads out from behind a big rock. "Hang on, Geronimo! **We'll save you!**" Thea called.

She pulled out a bottle of perfume. She sprayed it in the crab's eyes.

The crab blinked, confused. Then it swung me around in the air like a **CAT** with a new chew toy.

It was not a good feeling. **"GOODBYE, MOUSE WORLD!"** I sobbed. **"GOODBYE, FAMILY!"**

Just then, Trap hurled a coconut at the crab's head. Benjamin tickled it with a bird's feather.

The crab laughed and dropped me. Well, no, it didn't exactly drop me. It **hurled** me in the direction of the trees. I landed in the middle of a partridge nest. I was surrounded by a slew of open-mouthed tiny birds.

"HeeeeeeeeeLP!" I screamed.

Just at that moment, the mother partridge arrived. She had a big, fat worm in her beak.

47

I opened my mouth to scream. But before I could squeak, she dropped the worm into my mouth!

I spat it out in disgust. The mother partridge looked insulted.

"I am not a baby bird. My name is Stilton, *Geronimo Stilton*," I tried to explain.

The mother partridge just squawked. Then she pushed me out of the next. I landed with a thump on my head.

"Oh, why couldn't we go to the **Soft Squeak Resort**?" I moaned. I needed a nice cheese dinner. I needed a good night's rest. I needed an ice pack for **the lump on my head.**

THUMP ... FLOP!

That night, I was so tired, I fell right to sleep. At midnight, I woke up with a start. Something had woken me ... but what?

That's when I heard a very peculiar sound. **THUMP ... FLOP! THUMP ... FLOP! THUMP ... FLOP!**

It sounded like someone walking. But these were no ordinary pawsteps. A picture from the pirate guidebook flashed before my eyes – the ghost of Silverpaw. He had one good paw and one paw made of metal. I gulped. Was the ghost of Silverpaw really haunting **Thump Flop Island**?

Benjamin was awake, too. He grabbed my paw. "Uncle, maybe it's the **GHOST!**" he whispered.

I tried to look brave. "Don't worry, my dear little nephew," I said in my most confident voice. "I'll take care of it."

Now if only someone could take care of me. I felt faint with fear.

Cautiously, I trotted toward the beach.

Just as I'd thought. A long row of very strange pawprints dotted the sand. **Who could have left them?**

A Coconut on the Head!

Right then, I saw a large **SHADOW**.

"Yum, yummy yum, yummy yum yum!" it sang.

It was gnawing at a coconut.

I moved closer to get a better look. That's when it hit me. The coconut shell, that is. Yep, that ghost threw the shell right at my head. **HOLEY CHEESE!** That hurt!

I cried out in pain. Then I fainted. When I came to, the ghost was gone.

The next night, I heard the ghost shuffling around on the cliffs.

THUMP ... FLOP! THUMP ... FLOP! THUMP ... FLOP!

I knew I had to do something. So I crept up behind him. He was gnawing on a

roasted crab. I inched closer. **Oops!** The ghost spotted me. He took aim and launched the crab shell at me.

CLUNK! He hit me right between the ears. Nice shot. Could this be the ghost of a professional mouseball player? I thought it over for two second. Then I fainted.

The following night, I hid behind a sand dune. This time, I had a plan. I was going to **SURPRISE** the ghost. That's right. No more fainting for this mouse.

At the stroke of midnight, I heard his pawsteps.

THUMP ... FLOP! THUMP ... FLOP! THUMP ... FLOP!

This time, he was slurping on a mango. It was so strange. I had no idea ghosts liked to eat. I wondered if they sometimes ate the leftovers from my **MEGA-HUGE** fridge. I always blame Trap when my leftovers mysteriously disappeared. But maybe it was a **GHOST**! Now I would finally find out the truth.

I was getting excited. After all, I am a newspaper mouse. I like to get the scoop.

With a squeak, I jumped up from behind the sand

dune. "P-p-p-paws up!" I stammered. "D-d-don't move and you won't g-g-get hurt!" I hoped the ghosts couldn't tell I was petrified.

Seconds later, the pit of the mango caught me right between my eyes. I went down like a bowling pin.

When I came to, the ghost was leaning over me. His eyes glowed in the moonlight. Could it be? I blinked. Yes, it was. I was staring at **the ghost of Rough Rat Ricky – otherwise known as Bouncer!**

A GHOST

The ghost leaned toward me. "Yo, **Mousey Mouse**!" he shrieked at the top of his lungs.

I shook my head. Even as a ghost, **ROUGH RAT RICKY**, aka **BOUNCER**, was still just as loud. I was frightened out of my skull. **"B-B-B-BOUNCER, YOU'RE A G-G-GHOST!"** I squeaked.

I opened my eyes really wide. I have never seen a real live ghost before. Sure, I've had lots of near misses. Like when I was trapped in an old mansion that appeared to be **HAUNTED BY CATS**. Or when I was chased through subway tunnels by an oversized phantom. But this was the first time I'd ever been snout-to-snout with and honest-to-goodmouse **GHOST!**

My **FUR** stood on end. My knees felt weak. Then I noticed something strange. Bouncer wasn't floating in the air. And you couldn't see through his body. In fact, he looked just like he always did.

"Ho, ho, ho! I'm not ghost, **Mousey Mouse**!" Bouncer snickered. "You've been reading too many **spooky stories**!"

I watched as he stuffed his face with an entire pineapple. No, a ghost wouldn't eat food that way. But a real live **BOUNCER** would.

It turns out Bouncer had been living on the other side of the island. He had sprained his ankle when the plane crashed. He'd made a crutch to help him walk.

Can you guess what his pawsteps sounded like?

THUMP ... FLOP!
THUMP ... FLOP!
THUMP ... FLOP!

OYSTERS ON THE HALF SHELL

That night, we celebrated Bouncer's return with a **delicious** meal. Here's the menu:

Oysters (on the half shell)
Crab legs (minus the body)
Tuna (out of water)
Various fruits

I licked my whiskers. **CHEESECAKE!** I was so hungry, my tummy was rumbling in three different

languages. I decided to start with the oysters. But when I bit into one, I heard a horrifying **CRUNCH!**

"**SLIMY SWISS BALLS!**" I shrieked. I had chipped my tooth on something. I spat the nasty object into my paw. I could hardly believe my eyes. There in my paw lay an **ENORMOUSE** glittering white pearl!

Trap's eyes were shining with excitement. "We're rich! We're rich!" he sang. **"I knew you were good for something, Cousinkins!"**

ARE YOU A TEAM PLAYER?

The next morning, Trap woke me up at dawn. "Wake up, **Geronimoid**!" he shouted in my ear. "I've decided we need to go swimming. No, make that YOU need to go swimming." Uh-oh. I didn't like the sound of this.

"We need to find more oysters," Trap went on. "More oysters. More pearls. Got it, **Germeister**?"

I chewed my whiskers. "Why me?" I mumbled. "Why can't you go?"

Trap shook his head. "Well, isn't that just like you, Cousin? So self-centred. You need to learn to be a team player," he scolded. "Now, I've decided our jobs. You dive for the pearls. And I'll stay on the beach and watch."

I was too tired to argue. I grabbed a basket. Then I dived into the water. It was **freezing**. Oh, where was a nice, warm wet suit when you needed one?

I dived **DEEPER** and **DEEPER**. There were many tiny coloured fish around me. I swam by coral, sea anemones, starfish, octopuses, and more.

Finally, I spotted them.

Hundreds, no thousands, no gazillions

of oysters! I threw them into my basket. Then I swam to the surface.

Far away, I saw Trap waving his paws in the air. *What was my crazy cousin up to now?* I wondered. He was yelling something, but I couldn't understand a word of it.

It sounded like "**Shar** ... **shar** ..."

I rolled my eyes. He was probably telling me I need to share. Share the oysters. Share the pearls. Share the wealth. What kind of mouse did he think I was? Of course I would share these treasures with my family!

Just then, I noticed something out of the corner of my eye. **Ding!** A bell went off inside my brain. Trap wasn't lecturing me about sharing. He was warning me about a **GIANT SHARK!**

I began to swim like a maniac.

WATCH OUT FOR SHARKS!

The shark was so close, I could smell its **rotten breath**. Have you ever passed by the seafood section in a supermarket? That is exactly how it smelled. **Pee-yew!**

The shark had its mouth wide open. I could see its **RAZOR-SHARP TEETH** glinting in the sunlight. "Oh, please, don't eat me. I'm not fish food," I begged. "How about some nice tuna instead? Or maybe a couple of jellyfish?"

1. The shark was after me.

2. Bouncer dove in.

I didn't mean to pick on the other fish. But what could I do? I was **DESPERATE**.

Just then, I heard a scream. "I'll take care of it, **Mousey Mouse**!" a voice called.

I looked up. Bouncer was doing a cannonball off a high cliff. He landed right on the shark's back. **CRASH!** Instantly, the shark closed its eyes. Then it started snoring.

At last, I reached the beach. "It's about time," Trap snickered. He took the oysters. Then he gave me back the empty basket. "Off you go," he ordered. "And this time, you should really watch out for those sharks."

3. He threw himself on top of the shark.

4. Finally, I reached the beach.

63

THE OLD BOUNCER TREATMENT

That evening, Bouncer and I walked to the waterfall behind our camp. We each carried an empty coconut shell to collect water.

The sand around the waterfall **glistened** in the moonlight. I picked up a pawful. No, this wasn't any old beach sand. These were **quartz crystals!**

We were about to return to camp when we heard some voices. We peeked over the dune.

A broken-down canoe was nearing the beach. Two odd-looking mice were on board. The first was as thin as string cheese. He had **HUGE** buck teeth and was dressed in a moth-eaten captain's uniform. His sunglasses were held together by a plaster.

The other was as round as a ball of mozzarella. He wore a tiny sailor's hat and an old-fashioned one-piece black swimsuit. On two of his paws, he wore yellow flippers tied on with elastic bands.

While the chubby one rowed, he sang this tune:

"Treasure hunters are we!

"We sail across the sea.

"We search for jewellery and silver and gold,

"We lie and cheat and don't do what we're told.

"So get out of our way,

"Or we'll make you pay.

"Oh, treasure hunters are we!"

The chubby one looked **so excited**, he could hardly sit still. He bounced up and down like a yo-yo. The canoe rocked and swayed.

"No one gets in our way, right, Cape E. Tan? Right?" he squeaked. "We'll squish 'em. We'll squash 'em. We'll turn 'em into cat food. Right? **Right?**"

The captain snorted. "Less talking and more rowing, Chatterbox Charlie," he muttered.

But the chubby one kept on squeaking. "We can't tell anyone that we have the TREASURE MAP.

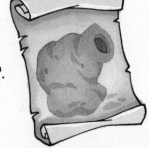

Right, Cap E. Tan? Right?" the chubby one babbled on.
"And we especially can't tell anyone that the **treasure
is hidden under a rock shaped like a cannon**.
Right, Cap E. Tan? Right?"

The captain stood with his paws on his hips.
"Quieeeeeeeeeeeeet!" he shrieked.

The chubby one blinked for two seconds. Then he
continued chattering on and on about the treasure.
"Where can it be? Oh, where, oh, where, oh, where?"
he jabbered.

The captain looked like
he was about to explode.
"ENOUGH!" he cried.

"Why don't you dive in and look for the rock? Or better yet, look for a muzzle!"

SPLASH! The chubby one hit the water. A few minutes later, he surfaced.

"No rocks shaped like a cannon! Just rocks shaped like rocks!" he announced.

The captain scratched his head. "Hmm, then we'll anchor by the island," he decided.

I grabbed Bouncer's paw. "What are we going to do now?" I whispered. Something told me these rodents weren't looking to make friends.

Bouncer was gnawing away on a hunk of pineapple. "I can always give them the old **BOUNCER TREATMENT, Mousey Mouse**," he offered.

I chewed my whiskers. "The old **BOUNCER TREATMENT**?" I asked.

"Sure," Bouncer snickered. "First I tie up their whiskers. Then I shave off their fur. Then ..."

I quickly shook my head. I wasn't into violence. That's no way to solve a problem. "We just need to get them off the island," I told Bouncer.

A GLITTERING WHITE GHOST

Bouncer cam up with a plan. "Wait for me here, **Mousey Mouse**," he said. Then he took off.

In the meantime, the two scoundrels had reached the island.

"Forward march!" ordered the captain.

The chubby one lit an oil lamp. He grabbed a shovel and started trudging through the sand.

I cringed. They were headed **straight for me**! But where was Bouncer?

Just then, I heard a rustling sound behind me.

A white **GHOST** emerged from the shadows. He was moaning, **"SCRAM! MOVE IT! GET LOST!"**

I opened my mouth to scream, but my vocal chords were frozen.

Then the ghost whispered in

my ear. "Pretty good, huh, **Mousey Mouse**?"

I should have known. It was just Bouncer. Before I could respond, he galloped down the path. **"SCRAAAAAAM! MOOOOOVE IT! GET LOOOOOST!"**

When the two crooks saw him, they turned white. **"A ghost!"** they cried.

They tore down the path and jumped into their canoe. They paddled away so fast, you'd think they were in a speedboat.

"I rolled in the quartz crystal sand," Bouncer told me. "Pretty cool, huh, **Mousey Mouse**?"

It was then that I noticed the crooks had lost their **TREASURE** map.

"Under the rock shaped like a cannon, the treasure is found," I read aloud.

I was curious. Was there really a **TREASURE**?

Bouncer scratched his head. "Err ... I'll bet my fur I've seen that rock **somewhere around here**," he mumbled.

DO YOU LOVE GOLD?

We decided to take a look. Bouncer searched everything on one side of the path. I searched the other.

I tiptoed into the dense bushes. My teeth were **chattering**. Who knew how many poisonous snakes were watching my every move, getting ready to bite me. Or strangle me. Or invite me to the family barbeque **as the main dish**!

I was about to turn back when I noticed a peculiar rock. **HOLEY CHEESE!** It was shaped just like a cannon. It was covered with moss and vines.

By the light of the moon, I could just make out words carved into the stone. It was a **strange riddle**.

DOES MY TREASURE MAKE YOU WANT TO SING?

DO YOU LOVE GOLD MORE THAN ANYTHING?

IF SO, THEN LOOK AROUND CAREFULLY.

NOTHING IS AS IT SEEMS, YOU SEE.

TAKE A SEAT AND LOOK AROUND.

WHATS THAT HIDING UNDERGROUND?

ONCE YOU FIND IT, YOU WILL SEE

MY TREASURE IS JUST LIKE A HOME TO ME,

I scratched my head. What could it mean? I sat down on a stone that looked like a seesaw to think. Suddenly, it began to move. A **big hole** opened up in the ground. Now, where did that lead? I am not a brave mouse, but my curiosity got to me. I decided to take a little peek. But as soon as I set my paw in the hole, **the stone closed over my head**. I was stuck like a rat in a trap!

"HeeeeLP!" I screeched. Oh, how do I always get myself into these terrifying situations. I'm a good mouse. I'm considerate. I help other rodents. I'm kind to mouselings. Well, the was that one time I pulled little Billy Bratfur's tail. But he asked for it. He was picking on my dear nephew Benjamin.

Bouncer's pawsteps broke into my thoughts. "Where are you, **Mousey Mouse**?" he called.

I jumped to my paws. **"UNDER HERE!"** I yelled. "Look for the trapdoor!"

"You lost your ear in a trapdoor?" Bouncer replied.

I began to chew my whiskers. "Sit on top of the stone seesaw!" I tried.

"Stone paw?" Bouncer said. "You found a paw?"

I hung my head in my paws. **RANCID RAT HAIRS!** We could go on like this forever. I'd be old and grey before Bouncer found that trapdoor. Just as I began to sob, the door opened.

"There you are, **Mousey Mouse**!" Bouncer cried. "Your ear looks fine. Now, where's that paw?"

Did You See
a Ghost?

Two strong paws reached down and pulled me out of the hole. It was my cousin Trap. Thea and Benjamin were right behind him. My screams of terror must have woken them up. Did I mention I'm afraid of the dark?

Meanwhile, Bouncer was jumping up and down with excitement. "What was under there, **Mousey Mouse**? You like a little pale. Did you see a ghost? Come on, let's go down."

He stuck a branch into the trapdoor to hold it open.

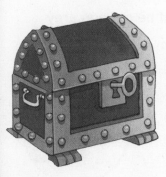

I was still frightened, but I have to admit, I was also curious. What was down below? A **TREASURE CHEST**? Bags of **GOLD**? Sparkling **gemstones**? A family of **GHOST PIRATES**?

I shivered. At least I had my family with me. My grandma Honeywhisker always said there's safety in numbers. If we ran into trouble, we could protect one another.

Together we gathered in front of the trapdoor. Bouncer led the way.

"Last one in is a **ROTTEN RODENT!**" Trap shrieked, pushing me ahead of him.

We headed down a very long staircase. *DOWN* ... *DOWN* ... *DOWN* ... we crept.

Bouncer led the way. He was holding a candle. The flickering light cast *spooky* shadows against the walls.

CHEWY CHEESE BITS! I was so scared, I stopped blinking.

Finally, we reached the end of the staircase. That's when I heard a rustling sound. Then warm, soft, hairy wings brushed against my fur. **That could only mean one thing ...**

A Bat!

"A BAT!" I squeaked. I flung my paws in the air. I guess that scared the bat. He got his claws tangled up in my fur. He seemed **frozen** with fear. I could feel his whole body *trembling*. I was *trembling*, too.

"Listen, just let go and we'll both be happy," I coaxed the bat. Instead, it hung on for dear life.

I groaned. This is what I got not taking Bat as a second language in school. No, I had taken Teddy Bear Hamster instead. And of course I never used it. How many Teddy Bear Hamsters do you know?

Benjamin's small voice cut into my thoughts. "**Hang on**, Uncle Geronimo. I'll help you!" he cried.

In a flash, he untangled the bat from my fur.

I was so relieved, I almost **FAINTED**.

Thea slapped me on the side of my snout. "Don't faint, **Gerry Berry**!" she commanded.

Trap was right behind her. "Don't faint, **Germeister**!" he agreed, slapping the other side of my snout.

Bouncer threw a pail of freezing water on my snout. "Don't faint, **Mousey Mouse**!" he bellowed.

I shook my head. "Enough!" I screamed. **"I feel fine!"**

At that instant, a stalactite hit me on the head like a bullet. **I was out cold before I even hit the ground.**

A LUMP AS BIG AS A
BALL OF MOZZARELLA!

When I came to, I felt the lump on my head. It was the size of a **giant ball of mozzarella**. I'm talking family-size portion.

Thea, Trap, Benjamin and Bouncer **RUSHED** to my side.

"He looks like he's about to faint again!" Thea shouted.

I quickly jumped to my paws. "I'm fine" I squeaked. No one was going to slap this mouse around again.

We continued on our way down a **dark**, rocky corridor. Suddenly, the passageway began to get light.

Finally, we reached the bottom.

"HOLEY CHEESE!" we all yelled

at once. We were in an immense

underground cavern filled with water. The walls were made of dazzling quartz crystals. The water below shimmered in their light. Coloured fish darted in and out. It was a **magical** sight.

But there was an even bigger surprise. At the centre of the cavern sat an **ENORMOUSE** galleon. It was a genuine PIRATE SHIP!

I could hardly believe my eyes. Then I noticed the name of the ship. It was called ... TREASURE. I took out the map and stared at it. "Under the rock shaped as a cannon, the treasure is found," I read aloud. I looked up at my family and Bouncer. **"CHEESECAKE!"** I squeaked. **"The ship is the treasure!"**

HEAVE ... HO!

With a **SPLASH**, Trap dived into the water. Nothing gets my cousin moving like the mention of treasure.

"Brrr ... the water's **freezing!**" he screeched as he paddled toward the ship. "Am I still moving? Am I still breathing? I can't event feel my own **FUR**!"

I rolled my eyes. *Trap really should consider becoming an actor,* I thought. He's the most **DRAMATIC** rodent I know.

When he reached the ship, Trap lowered a small ladder for the rest of us to climb.

"Now we can sail home!" Thea squeaked.

Meanwhile, Bouncer and trap tried to lift the anchor.

HEAVE ... HO!
HEAVE ... HO!

It was so heavy it wouldn't budge.

A galleon was a warship or a cargo ship with various decks. It had three or four masts with square sails. It sailed during the fifteenth, sixteenth and seventeenth centuries and was suitable for long voyages.

But just at that moment, something totally strange happened. The ship began moving **all by itself**! The masts rose into the air. Minutes later, the galleon drifted out of the mouth of the cavern and headed out to sea!

Was the ship **HAUNTED**? Or was there some logical explanation? There was no time to think about it. I ran to help trap and Thea with the sails. The ship shot off like a cat in an attic full of mice.

"Want me to be the pilot?" Bouncer asked, reaching for the steering wheel.

"Noooo!" we all shouted at once. Thea pushed Bouncer aside and grabbed the wheel. "I'll handle this," she said.

Meanwhile, Benjamin was busy drawing a sketch on a banana leaf. It showed a picture of a PIRATE SHIP in its secret hiding place.

"That's very good, Nephew," I told him.

Benjamin beamed. "I just had the best idea, Uncle," he said. "You can use it in your next book."

"What book?" I asked. It felt like years since I had sat down at my desk to write.

"The book about this adventure," Benjamin grinned.

Hmmm … a book about deserted island, pirate ship and treasure. Maybe Benjamin was right. **It did sound like an exciting story.**

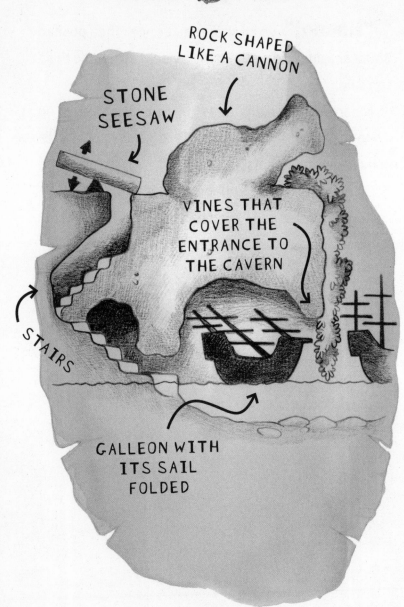

THE ISLAND'S LAST SECRET

The ship glided off into the warm southerly winds. The breeze felt great **RIPPLING** through my fur. It felt good to be out on the open sea. I guess I'd had enough of **THUMP FLOP ISLAND**. I was looking forward to going home.

I took one last look at the island. That's when I head the sound. No, it wasn't a seagull squawking. It wasn't a monkey chattering. It sounded like ...

THUMP ... FLOP! THUMP ... FLOP!

I gulped. Was it the ghost of Silverpaw? Did he really live on **THUMP FLOP ISLAND**?

I smiled under my whiskers. I guess everyone has a right to a secret. **Even an island!**

SILVERPAW'S SHIP LOG

By now, the island was far behind us. Thea quickly began to **bark** out orders.

"Trap, you'll do the cooking. Bouncer, you'll be in charge of the sails. Benjamin, you'll keep the cabins neat and tidy. And Geronimo, you'll search for the navigational controls," she commanded.

"AYE AYE, CAPTAIN," Trap muttered sarcastically. But he hopped to it when Thea looked at him. My sister can be a little scary when she wants to be.

I headed for the pirate's cabin. There were swords and sabres hanging on the walls. An oil painting glared at me. It was a picture of the pirate Silverpaw.

How **strange**. For some reason, he looked so familiar.

I opened the desk drawer. So many papers! What

a mess. Old Silverpaw really needed a secretary. Thank goodness for my secretary, Mousella. Without her, I would never get anything done at The Rodent's Gazette. She keeps me organised.

I leafed through the logbook. It showed all of the voyages the ship had taken. It also mentioned the **TONNES AND TONNES OF GOLD** seized.

I wondered where all of that gold was now.

Then I found a family album of sorts. When I opened it, I could hardly believe my eyes.

On one of the pages was written the name **Stilton!**

Something Familiar

I kept reading. And I soon discovered that the great-great-great-great-grandfather of my great-grandfather was a cousin of the pirate Silverpaw!

JUMPING GERBIL BABIES!

That meant I had pirate blood in my veins. I glanced at the picture of Silverpaw. For a second, I wondered what I would look like with an eye patch. Maybe I could try one on when I got home. Geronimo the pirate. I sort of liked the sound of it. It made me feel **ROUGH** and **RUGGED**. Not at all like my usual self.

"Have you found the controls yet? What's taking you so long, **CHEESEBRAIN?!**" my sister screeched.

89

I raced upstairs. So much for rough and rugged. I couldn't wait to tell Trap, Thea and Benjamin what I'd discovered.

My relatives seemed proud to have PIRATE BLOOD in their veins.

We were still talking about pirates when Benjamin interrupted us.

"Come look!" he called. He had finished polishing the ship's brass fixtures. They were **BRILLIANT**!

In fact, they looked as if they we made of ... GOLD!

"CHEESECAKE!" Trap squeaked. "It is gold!"

Yes, everything on the ship was made of

GOLD. The door handles, the taps, the pots – even the anchor!

So that was why the ship was called TREASURE. It really was worth its weight in gold!

I proposed donating the ship to the National Mouseum of new Mouse City in the name of the Stilton family. "It is an important moment in our family's history," I explained. "It will be great to share it with all the rodents on Mouse Island."

Our past, for good or for bad, belongs to us. We need to know it in order to know ourselves better.

BLACK CLOUDS ON THE HORIZON

The following morning, I found Bouncer and Trap in the kitchen. Trap was cooking and Bouncer was eating. Well, I guess you could call it eating. He looked more like a food processor stuck on high speed. Bouncer was shovelling food into his mouth **SO FAST**, his paws were a blur.

"Yo, **Mousey Mouse**," he called to me. "Your cousin and I have decided to open a seafood restaurant when we get home." He held up a soupspoon with what looked like some oysters on it. "Want to taste?" he asked.

I shook my head. The last time I ate seafood cooked by my cousin, I got horribly **SICK**. I was in the bathroom half the night. And I wasn't reading the newspaper, if you know what I mean.

PIRATE SOUP

INGREDIENTS FOR 4 MICE:

4 pounds cleaned clams and oysters

3 tablespoons oil

½ onion, chopped

2 glaric cloves

4 tomatoes, peeled and chopped

Toasted mini bread slices

Parsley

PREPARATION: In a skillet, sauté the onion and garlic in oil until transparent. Add the tomato and parsley. Sprinkle salt and pepper, to taste. After a few minutes, add the clams and oysters. Cook over a high heat until all the shellfish are opened. Place some slices of toast on each soup bowl, then pour in the soup.

A SUGGESTION FOR TRUE PIRATES:

Add some hot peppers to the dish!

I left the kitchen and found Thea in Silverpaw's cabin. She was busy studying ancient nautical charts to plot out our route.

Just then, Benjamin ran into the room. "Uncle Geronimo, **BLACK CLOUDS** on the horizon!"

We raced up to the deck. Thea shook her head worriedly. "Looks like a real *STORM* is brewing!" she confirmed.

We lowered the sails and substituted them with smaller ones. Now if the wind blew really hard, the ship would not pick up too much speed. We closed the portholes to prevent **WATER** from seeping in. Then we tied ourselves to the side of the ship to keep from being blown overboard.

Did I mention **I hate bad weather?** It can be so wild. It can be so crazy. It can be so hard on your **FUR**. Once I got caught in a downpour before I was about to give a speech. I was so embarrassed. What a **BAD FUR DAY**.

To keep our spirits up, Bouncer and trap told us some sailor jokes. I must have been delirious because

I thought they were funny.

SAILOR JOKES

Captain: Throw out the anchor!
Sailor: But, sir, it's still new!

A leak springs aboard a ship.
The captain arrives.
Unfortunately, its already too late.
The ship is about to sink.
The captain shouts at the cabin boy,
"Cabin boy! When you saw that the
water was coming in, you
should have called me, fool!"
The cabin boy looks surprised.
"But, Captain," he protests.
"It's not right to be rude.
I would never
call you fool."

STILTON SINKS!!

By now, the sky had turned **black as night**. The wind was blowing **FURIOUSLY**.

The waves were as high as the Sky Rat Tower Bistro in New Mouse City. Rodents pay lots of money to eat there. You can see the whole city from its incredible rooftop terrace. Of course, the Sky Rat is not for me. I get a little queasy when I'm up in high places.

I was thinking about the Sky Rat as the ship bounced up and down on the water. My stomach was bouncing up and down, too. I felt as **GREEN** as a piece of **mouldy cheese!**

At that moment, a sail split in two.

"We need to take it down!" Bouncer shouted. He quickly leaped onto the bridge.

"I'll stay here with the women and children," Trap announced.

Reluctantly, I followed Bouncer. The ship titled **dangerously** to one side. Oh, what a way to go! Washed overboard into the wild ocean waves. I could just read the headlines:

STILTON SINKS IN THE SOUTHERN SEAS! POPULAR NEWSPAPER PUBLISHER ALL WASHED UP! WHAT A TRAGEDY.

Still, there was no time to cry about it now. I had a job to do helping Bouncer.

At last, we were able to lower the split sail. I had just breathed a sigh of relief when something even more **TERRIFYING**

97

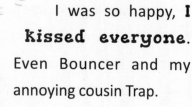

happened. The rope holding my dear sweet nephew snapped in two. **Benjamin was sliding into the sea!**

I rushed towards him. I was able to grab his paw, but he was slipping fast. **SLIMY SWISS BALLS!** We were both falling snout-first into the ocean!

Then a **HUGE HAIRY PAW** appeared out of nowhere. It grabbed me by the scruff of the neck. In fact, it picked us both up. Bouncer grinned. "No time for swimming, **Mousey Mice**," he said with a chuckle. "In case you haven't noticed, there's a terrible storm going on!"

At last, the sky began to clear.

"The worst is over!" my sister announced. "The storm is passing."

I was so happy, **I kissed everyone**. Even Bouncer and my annoying cousin Trap.

WONDERFUL, FABUMOUSE MOUSE ISLAND!

Finally, one morning we spotted an island. Oh, I'm not talking about any old island. This was the **best** island on the whole planet. **WONDERFUL, FABUMOUSE MOUSE ISLAND!**

We drifted past the Statue of Liberty holding up her piece of cheese. Today she seemed to be smiling right at us. Ah, it felt so good to be home at last!

I glanced at the others. Even Trap had tears in his eyes. After one big group hug, we twisted our tails together and shouted, **"Nothing can stop the Stilton family!"**

The crowd on land stared at us open-mouthed. I guess we must have looked strange. After all, it's not

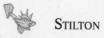

every day a PIRATE SHIP sails into New Mouse City Harbour.

"We are donating this pirate ship of Silverpaw's and its precious cargo to the good rodents of New Mouse City!" I announced.

Everyone clapped.

"HURRAH for the Stilton family! HURRAH for new Mouse City!" they cheered.

A SURPRISE
TELEPHONE CALL

Do you want to know how it all ended?

Silverpaw's ship became a splendid floating museum. It was dedicated to the **history of pirates**.

Old mice and young came to visit. Yes, it was quite the tourat attraction. Trap bought a pirate costume and gave pirate tours for a small fee. Leave it to my cousin to cash in on our good fortune.

Thea decided to take another holiday. Guess where she ended up this time? **The Soft Squeak Resort**. Of course, she had a fantastic time. There's nothing like the Squeak for a **relaxing getaway**. And knowing my sister, she probably met dozens and dozens of admirers there.

As for me, I was thrilled to go back to work. No more

dangerous adventures for me. **I'm too fond of my tail.**

One day, I got a call. "Yo, **Mousey Mouse**!" a voice squeaked on the other end. "It's your old pal, **ROUGH RAT RICKY**, aka **BOUNCER**. Listen, I'm coming to visit you."

All of a sudden, I felt a giant headache coming on.

"My mum can't wait to meet you. And my twelve little cousins are so excited, they can hardly sit still," he continued. "Better stock up on the cheese, though. These crazy rascals will **eat you out of house and hole!**"

I tried to squeak. But no sound came out. Stars swam before my eyes. Bouncer and his whole family were coming to stay with me? There was only one thing to do. **I fainted.**

ABOUT THE AUTHOR

Born in New Mouse City, Mouse Island, GERONIMO STILTON is Rattus Emeritus of Mousomorphic Literature and of Neo-Ratonic Comparative Philosophy. For the past twenty years, he has been running The Rodent's Gazette, New Mouse City's most widely read daily newspaper.

Stilton was awarded the Ratitzer Prize for his scoops on *The Curse of the Cheese Pyramid* and *The Search for Sunken Treasure*. He has also received the Andersen Prize

for Personality of the Year. His works have been published all over the globe.

In his spare time, Mr. Stilton collects antique cheese rinds and plays golf. But what he most enjoys is telling stories to his nephew Benjamin.

THE RODENT'S GAZETTE

1. Main entrance
2. Printing presses (where everything is printed)
3. Accounts department
4. Editorial room (where editors, illustrators, and designers work)
5. Geronimo Stilton's office
6. Geronimo's botanical garden

MAP OF NEW MOUSE CITY

1. Industrial Zone
2. Cheese Factories
3. Angorat International Airport
4. WRAT Radio and Television Station
5. Cheese Market
6. Fish Market
7. Town Hall
8. Snotnose Castle
9. The Seven Hills of Mouse Island
10. Mouse Central Station
11. Trade Centre
12. Movie Theatre
13. Gym
14. Catnegie Hall
15. Singing Stone Plaza
16. The Gouda Theatre
17. Grand Hotel
18. Mouse General Hospital
19. Botanical Gardens
20. Cheap Junk for Less (Trap's store)
21. Parking Lot
22. Mouseum of Modern Art
23. University and Library
24. The Daily Rat
25. The Rodent's Gazette
26. Trap's House
27. Fashion District
28. The Mouse House Restaurant
29. Environmental Protection Centre
30. Harbour Office
31. Mousidon Square Garden
32. Golf Course
33. Swimming Pool
34. Blushing Meadow Tennis Courts
35. Curlyfur Island Amusement Park
36. Geronimo's House
37. Historic District
38. Public Library
39. Shipyard
40. Thea's House
41. New Mouse Harbour
42. Luna Lighthouse
43. The Statue of Liberty
44. Hercule Poirat's Office
45. Petunia Pretty Paws's House
46. Grandfather William's House

MAP OF MOUSE ISLAND

1. Big Ice Lake
2. Frozen Fur Peak
3. Slipperyslopes Glacier
4. Coldcreeps Peak
5. Ratzikistan
6. Transratania
7. Mount Vamp
8. Roastedrat Volcano
9. Brimstone Lake
10. Poopedcat Pass
11. Stinko Peak
12. Dark Forest
13. Vain Vampires Valley
14. Goosebumps Gorge
15. The Shadow Line Pass
16. Penny-Pincher Castle
17. Nature Reserve Park
18. Las Ratayas Marinas
19. Fossil Forest
20. Lake Lake
21. Lake Lakelake
22. Lake Lakelakelake
23. Cheddar Crag
24. Cannycat Castle
25. Valley of the Giant Sequoia
26. Cheddar Springs
27. Sulphurous Swamp
28. Old Reliable Geyser
29. Vole Vale
30. Ravingrat Ravine
31. Gnat Marshes
32. Munster Highlands
33. Mousehara Desert
34. Oasis of the Sweaty Camel
35. Cabbagehead Hill
36. Rattytrap Jungle
37. Rio Mosquito
38. Mousefort Beach
39. San Mouscisco
40. Swissville
41. Cheddarton
42. Mouseport
43. New Mouse City
44. Pirate Ship of Cats

HAVE YOU READ ALL OF GERONIMO'S ADVENTURES?

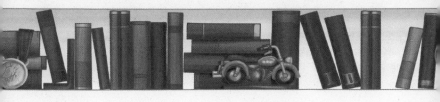

HAPPY READING!